SPEED

by R. R. Knudson

with photographs by Linda Eber

A SKINNY BOOK
E. P. DUTTON   NEW YORK

Text copyright © 1983 by R. R. Knudson
Illustrations copyright © 1983 by Linda Eber

Library of Congress Cataloging in Publication Data

Knudson, R. Rozanne, date
Speed.
(A Skinny book)
Summary: A black high school track star depends on
speed in his legs to make him forget the pain of breaking
up with his girl.
[1. Track and field—Fiction]   I. Eber, Linda, ill.
II. Title.
PZ7.K785Sp   1983   [Fic]   82-21009
ISBN 0-525-44052-6

Published in the United States by E. P. Dutton, Inc.,
2 Park Avenue, New York, N.Y. 10016

Published simultaneously in Canada by Clarke,
Irwin & Company Limited, Toronto and Vancouver

Editor: Ann Durell   Designer: Isabel Warren-Lynch

Printed in the U.S.A.   First Edition
10 9 8 7 6 5 4 3 2 1

7056741

The baton used in the photos of SPEED is the one with which a new world record was set for the 880-yard relay on May 13, 1967. That relay was won by the San Jose State team in 1:21.1 (1 minute, 21 seconds, and $^1/_{10}$ of a second). The four members of the team were Bob Talmadge, Ken Shackleford, Lee Evans, and Tommie Smith (whose anchor leg was 19.6—19 seconds and $^6/_{10}$ of a second). Their names appear on the baton.

"Stick!"

"Take the stick, Tyrone."

"Come on, brother. Practice taking hold the stick."

"Why you being so raggedy, man?"

Every boy on the relay team yelled at Tyrone.

But Tyrone wasn't having any. He didn't grab the stick. He kept his right hand rolled up in an air-tight fist. He kept his mind on how much he hated all these guys.

Hate. For-real hate, he thought.

"Please, Tyrone. Please practice taking the baton pass." His coach yelled, too.

1

And another thing. He hated this coach who was trying to hand him the relay baton. What was going on around here, anyway? A woman track coach at Watts High School? She couldn't help him run faster.

Tyrone was angry. You could tell how angry from his narrow-slit eyes. His eyes said, "Stop the team. I want to get off."

Nobody's eyes were as mean as Tyrone's. Not even the eyes of Hitler.

Never mind eyes. Tyrone's fists got ready to punch out anybody who stepped into his running lane. Oh, hate felt good to him. Hate made him run faster today. He ran out of the passing zone and halfway around the track.

"Later on, eggheads," he called.

He left three teammates and the coach in his dust.

There wasn't all that much dust at Watts High School. The track had been rolled and watered. It felt smooth. It was definitely fast. OOWEEE. Tyrone's feet loved every one of his fast strides around the track. His feet kissed the track.

Only his feet remembered how a kiss felt.

He hated everything else, everybody else.

Tyrone felt love and hate at the same time. He slowed to think of which he felt most. His running body felt almost happy. His arms and legs did exactly what he asked them to do. Moving around the track kept him from thinking. And he didn't want to think about his past.

His mind felt angry. He heard Coach calling, "Tyrone, please." He hated her.

The team captain called, "Over here, turkey. Practice how Coach Huey shows you."

"She shows me nothing," Tyrone told himself out loud. He stopped—just like that. He let his arms go dead. He dragged his feet walking back to his teammates. He sat down on a bench.

Coach called, "Now why do you want to ruin our practice?"

He shot her the mean Tyrone-glance.

"Has it sunk in yet that your best time for 400 meters is 46 seconds? You're the fastest pair of legs on the team. Probably the fastest high-school runner in Los Angeles."

Tyrone didn't bother to shrug. His eyes said, "So what?"

"And yet you won't try. Just then, you did one lap in four minutes. Four." She held up four fingers. "How will we beat Santa Monica High with only three relay legs? We need an anchor leg who will take the stick and run his heart out."

"We can't beat Santa Monica," Tyrone said. "So what?" His voice was as flat as the track.

Coach Lynda Huey walked past Tyrone. "You couldn't get away with being so rude if you weren't so fast," she said with disgust. "You know we need your speed next week."

Speed, Tyrone thought. My speed is what counts. Speed is all that matters to a coach. It's all that matters to me. Speed here, speed there, speed every olé which way. All I got anymore is my speed.

Life in the fast lane. He couldn't live anywhere else. He'd die if he couldn't run faster and faster.

His teammates stood grinning at him. They hid their real feelings because they, too, needed his speed. They must win races to call attention to themselves. They had to get what they wanted, same as Coach Huey. And they wanted a lot.

But they hated Tyrone for sure.
The feeling was mutual.

Look at this relay team photo from the Watts High yearbook.

No, don't just look. Study it. The photo makes it easy to understand this story about four teammates. Easy to know their lives.

Take Tyrone, for starters. He's sitting apart from the others. The photographer yelled at him to move in, but Tyrone stayed put. He didn't want to touch them. That's why he won't take the stick from his teammates. He's afraid when they're so near him they'll somehow touch his hand.

Tyrone's a loner. He wasn't always, but he is now.

And check out what he's wearing. His coach asked him to wear his track uniform. When she asked, Tyrone said nothing. Now the photo says it all. He didn't even bother to put on one of his socks.

The other boys on the relay team really like Tyrone's pose. They like how his eyes point away from them. No way those eyes can blast them from this page of the Watts yearbook. Secretly they wish his hood covered his whole body.

Next to Tyrone—if you can call it next to—sits Hollywood Johnson with his comb. The teammate in front of Hollywood, the one staring straight at the camera, is Ron. He's serious. He's captain of the relay team. And next to Ron is Luther Junior, looking down at his uncomfortable hands.

Luther looks nice, and he is.

He looks worried, and he is. That's because he thinks he's wasting time by posing for the yearbook. He wants all his time to train harder, because he hopes to win a college scholarship for running.

Luther has his whole life planned. First, he runs fast with these guys, who make him look faster. They win big—the City Championship. Then a college coach will notice Luther. Bingo! It's UCLA time.

Then Luther runs track for UCLA. Off the track he studies, studies. He goes on to be a doctor, saving lives and all that: Doctor Luther Williams, Junior.

He's worried until then.

You can see it in his hands. How will those hands hold on to a knife in the hospital? They're so shaky right now that he drops the baton on lots of passes. "The bad hands," his coach calls him—but she likes him anyway.

So does the team captain. "Stay cool, my man," Ron tells Luther during practice.

Luther Junior doesn't hear. He's thinking of his whole life at once: Faster . . . UCLA . . . operations on people's hearts . . . I need the good hands.

Ron's hands tell us a different story. He's confident. He knows his hands are like glue on the stick. After all, he's team captain. He believes in his brothers. His team could be Number One in Los Angeles. Next week they could blow away Santa Monica High School without working up a sweat. In June, they could win the City Championship.

Ron's a believer.

Also a ladies' man. You can tell from the ring he wears.

That ring didn't just drop off the moon. It was a gift. It's worth a lot. When he takes the stick in a race, it clicks against his ring and reminds him of his latest girlfriend. She makes his legs stride faster.

Ron's sitting in the photo wishing all his ex-girlfriends could be there with their arms around him. The photographer should have reminded him to smile at them.

That poor photographer spent most of his time warning Hollywood to stop combing his hair, stop pulling his uniform an inch this way or that way.

"Hollywood's wanting to make this his first movie," Ron explained.

The photographer didn't have all day. "Don't try to get the sun to gleam off your gold chain," he begged Hollywood.

"I'm your star." Hollywood flashed his perfect teeth. "Let the sun shine on me and me alone." Hollywood's voice had charm.

"Four stars is here," Ron took over and said, "me, Luther Junior, Tyrone, and you."

The photographer looked like he might toss his camera at the Watts High relay team.

"Sit still," he begged Hollywood.

"Smile—that boy in the hood. What's hurting you?" he asked Tyrone. "I'm counting to three. One, two—" The camera clicked before "three." Before Tyrone could move further away.

And before Coach Lynda Huey could force herself to sit beside the boys. She's down on the track, asking herself aloud: "Will these four ever start acting like they're on the same team?"

3

You think the team had problems with their yearbook photo? That's nothing! You should see them running their training hill.

Every Tuesday in April and May, they go up that hill five times, hot or not, tired or not. They don't do it for fun, either. It's painful to run up. They do it only to strengthen their gear boxes— their thighs and buttocks. Coach Huey makes them run up the half-mile hill, turn and run down, turn and run up. She works them until their tongues hang out.

But first they have to ride to the hill. The Watts section of Los Angeles is flat. The team must ride the freeway across L.A. to the killer hill that Coach Huey chose for them.

That means they sit together in Coach's VW for a half hour.

"Move over" are Tyrone's only words on the freeway. He pretends to be asleep.

Hollywood looks into the mirror and practices his future roles on TV. He hopes his relay team will win big enough to put him on the sports news. When that happens, Hollywood has it made, because a TV big shot will see his pretty face.

"You and me, baby," Hollywood sings in the car. "This is one song I'll do with Donna Summer on the tube."

Coach Huey parks in the UCLA parking lot.

"Get out of the car, turkey." Ron calls everyone "turkey."

Hollywood and his comb are out almost before the car stops. He is definitely no turkey.

The coach puts the boys through their warm-ups on the practice field. "Stretch," she tells them.

Luther stretched, pretending the UCLA coach was watching him.

Hollywood hoped to be seen running Sunset Hill by a big shot. He warmed up to make his body shine with sweat—shine like a star.

One of Ron's girlfriends always waited at the top of the hill to cheer him with her eyes and to kiss him at the turnaround. So the faster Ron warmed up, the faster to a kiss.

"Stretch your hamstrings good," Coach Huey warned. She showed them how.

She'd chosen Sunset from a hundred hills in L.A. She knew it would be hard training. But she also knew each boy had a reason to run his best there.

"Everybody ready?" she asked. "Get set."

Tyrone moved his sweatband so it didn't cover his eyes.

"Go."

Tyrone broke first from the starting line. After 100 yards, he was still in first place. After 200 yards—250 yards—Tyrone held first as the team went out of sight.

The hill curved. Coach Huey wouldn't see them again until they ran down.

She watched cars go up Sunset Hill with ease. "Easy as Tyrone makes sprinting seem," she said to herself.

When Tyrone came back in sight, he still led the pack. He looked fresh. Mean, but fresh. His teammates looked tired. Coach Huey had to push them off the starting line.

"Go. Go."

They went this time and the third time up Sunset Hill.

But then, the fourth time Coach Huey tried to send them up, no one ran except Tyrone.

Coach pointed to the lipstick on Ron's chin. "Go for it," she urged.

She pointed to the UCLA track, which was below them where they stood on the hill.

"Would you say no to the UCLA coach, Luther?"

She told Hollywood, "Donna Summer lives near here and might be riding by in her BMW."

These psych-ups worked. The guys took off and gave the hill what they had left: their willpower. Their legs were gone, but their brains kept them moving.

"Run!" said their brains—and they did.

But not again. Not the fifth time.

"No way we running." Ron spoke for them all. They sat down under a tree.

"Move over," Tyrone said.

They sat and sweat and moaned and swore not to move.

"You run it, Coach," Hollywood said as a joke.

"Drag Tyrone up with you," Ron said to see what Tyrone would do.

Coach Huey pulled off her warm-up suit. The team had never seen her in shorts. Right then Hollywood knew for sure she could run. He knew how speed looked in the legs.

She yelled, "Take your mark, Tyrone." She jumped off the line. She was in the lead 100 yards before Tyrone stood up. He'd have to use his gear box to catch her.

The other boys followed on the run. They moved as fast as their curiosity would take them. They forgot their pain as they ran up the hill. They wanted to see Coach Huey beat Tyrone to the top. At the turnaround, Ron forgot to pause for his kiss.

"Hey, come on back here," screamed his new girlfriend, Deneen.

Down, down one last time today. Coach Huey flew. She hadn't set a U.S.A. sprint record for nothing. Tyrone didn't pass her until she let him on the final stride.

When Luther Junior crossed the finish line, he slapped the coach a high five with one of his bad hands.

"And then what?"

"Coach Huey almost beat the turkey," Ron told all the weight lifters listening.

"Huey ran faster? Didn't Tyrone quit your team after that?" a baseball player from Los Angeles City College asked. He worked out with these track boys every day. He'd heard all about Tyrone.

"Tyrone hasn't quit us yet," Hollywood announced in his TV voice. "He ran his fastest lap at today's practice."

The relay team was training in the LACC weight room with a bunch of athletes from colleges around there. Ron lay on a bench doing presses. Hollywood lifted his dumb-bell—in front of the mirror, of course. He was the only one smiling. A girl from the LACC volley-ball team lifted weights behind him.

Luther and the baseball player were doing squats.

"When's your track meet with Santa Monica?" the baseball player asked.

"This Saturday," Luther answered tensely.

Hollywood added, "We'll find out Saturday if Tyrone will take the stick and turn on his speed. Stay tuned to this station." He was joking, but he sounded nervous.

Luther joined the gossip on his break from squatting. "You ever notice Tyrone's hands? How they won't touch anything—just the stick?"

"His hands is lonely," Ron said, "if they don't touch nothing."

Hollywood reminded Luther, "He never drops the stick once he does take it."

"Those things is all we knows about him." Ron began his third set of presses.

"Except we know he skips weight work and hates us and—"

"Hates Coach Huey worse." A shout went up in the weight room.

"We did, too. Remember when she first showed up last month?" Hollywood asked his teammates.

"Yeah. Told her quick find her a disappearing act to do." Ron laughed.

They remembered how at first they refused to train her way. They didn't want a substitute coach. They wanted their old coach back from the hospital. When Coach Huey tried to time their sprints, the team—except Tyrone—limped around the track instead of running. But then Ron read in an old magazine how Huey had set an American sprint record.

Ron reminded the team, "I asked her was it true she champ. She say, 'Yeah,' and then jammed us up about workouts. She made us run! She say she coach us to an American high school record in the 4×400-meter relay."

"I sure began to like her that day," Luther confessed. "She's taught me how to run my 100 meters faster."

"She okay with me if she help us win. My Stacy sure do love a winner." Ron moved from the bench to the bar-bell rack.

"Me too." Luther Junior hung on to his dumb-bell for a change.

"Whew, enough. Or I'll be too stiff for Santa Monica. Let's do some posing." Hollywood flexed his muscles in front of the mirror and sang out with "H-O-L-L-Y."

Towels flew at him.

Hollywood ducked. He acted like Tyrone,

with Tyrone's mean eyes and low voice. "Don't touch me."

"Why can't we touch you, Tyrone?" Luther asked.

Hollywood was a good actor, but he couldn't answer for Tyrone, the mystery runner.

Speed? Yes. Tyrone had it. And hate.

Anything else? Who knows about Tyrone? He had just transferred to Watts High in February.

"We don't even know if he eats or sleeps," said Hollywood to his mirror self.

"I see him running at night sometimes," Luther said.

"Where?"

"On my way home from the library. He's always alone."

The room became silent. You could hear showers dripping. All these human beings, and no one had another word to say about Tyrone. No teammate knew his secret.

Never mind. If Tyrone ran against Santa Monica on Saturday, they'd win. That's what mattered.

Tyrone ran.

He even wore half his uniform. His sweatband covered his ears, not his eyes, but he could hear Coach Huey.

"Check your spikes. Tighten them," she warned her team long before their race.

They sat together where they had made camp near the track. They stretched and listened to Coach. For fun, they listened to Donna on Hollywood's box. For practice, they passed the stick around in a circle.

Tyrone didn't reach for the stick, but he did let Ron press it into his fist. When it came time for the team to jog together, Tyrone shot out ahead. Yet later he warmed up his hamstrings with Coach close to him and counting.

"One, two, three." *Clap.* "Left, center, right." *Clap.* "Watts High. Watts High," Coach Huey counted and clapped for pep.

Tyrone told himself to hang tight. The only good part of life was coming. The part that kept him alive. Speed was coming soon—his own speed.

"Speed will save me," Tyrone said aloud.

When he ran, he forgot. The faster he ran, the more he forgot.

Speed kills. It killed Tyrone's pain.

The 4×400-meter relay would be the last race of this meet with Santa Monica. It was time to head for the starting line. Lynda Huey gave each boy some final coaching.

"Luther, you're running first. Come out of the blocks hard. Hold on to the stick hard. Ron, you take the pass from Luther. If you're behind Santa Monica, don't try to catch up on the first turn. You have 400 meters to catch up. Don't die early."

"No way I die in front of Wanda and Melody and . . ."

"Hollywood, remember your form. Running

form is the key when you get tired. Form is all you have left in the race."

Coach turned next to Tyrone.

He didn't hear what she said. He was thinking aloud. "Speed is all I got left in my whole life. I forget Val when I run." He caught himself.

But there! He'd said it. He'd almost yelled about his old girlfriend. Listen up, Watts High relay team. You'll learn why Tyrone's unhappy and angry.

The team was too busy to listen.

Luther walked to the starting line and settled his feet into the blocks. His right hand held the stick. He coiled his body, waiting for

"Set!"

The gun went off and so did Luther. For 47 seconds on that track, he did everything right. He sped into the passing zone well ahead of the Santa Monica runner. Ron was waiting there with his hand raised for the stick.

What stick?

Luther had dropped it, just then as he pushed it toward Ron's hand.

Their stick lay in the dirt.

Until Ron grabbed it up. It rubbed against his ring. Then the stick was on its way around the track again.

Ron didn't panic. "Be cool, be cool," he told himself on the run. "My ladies is watching me." He passed the stick to Hollywood.

"Stroke, stroke," Hollywood ordered himself on the run. "I'm catching him. Santa Monica's only ten meters ahead of me. Damn that Luther for dropping."

No time to think about his pretty face on TV! Hollywood took the second curve too wide. He saw Tyrone waiting with an upheld fist. Would the fist open?

"Stick!"

Tyrone took it and ran. Not because he wanted to catch up. He didn't care who won this race or any race. Or who dropped or who watched from the crowd. Unless Valery was watching. Unless Val followed him with her eyes around the first curve and into the back straight.

She wasn't there, Tyrone knew in his exploding heart.

One more curve to run. Tyrone sped to forget. The Santa Monica runner was five meters ahead, four meters, three.

Tyrone forgot Val at this speed.

His mind went blank. His heart stopped beating Val's name and worked to send rivers of blood to his muscles. Screams from the crowd couldn't break into his peace of mind.

He ran faster than he ever had before.

He *almost* caught the Santa Monica runner at the finish line.

After the race, Luther Junior knelt on the track and cried his eyes out.

Ron hung on to Sherri while he bad-mouthed Luther for dropping the stick. "Turkey" was the nicest word he called poor Luther.

Hollywood watched the anchor man on Santa Monica's team talking to some man with a tape recorder. Hollywood felt so bad he covered his head with a towel.

Tyrone ran around and around the track they'd just lost on. Each time he passed Luther, Tyrone told him to forget about dropping the stick. "No one remembers," he said.

"I made us lose." Luther beat his hands against the clay track.

"Get up, Luther Junior," Tyrone said. "Forget. Forget."

Tyrone wished he could follow his own advice. If only he could forget the breakup with Val. If he could just wipe her out of his mind by wiping his hand across his eyes. Or by covering his eyes forever.

"Shake it off," Tyrone said to Luther, who seemed in worse shape than Tyrone was himself.

Then, without thinking, Tyrone leaned over and pulled Luther up from the track. They walked back to the team bus and listened to Coach Huey's plans for next week's practice.

She said, "Monday, stick work."

She said, "Tuesday, stick work."

"Luther's stick work. His bad hands is fixing to keep us out of the Championships," Ron called.

Coach Huey insisted: "*Our* stick work and *our* curve running and *our* starts and *our* speed. We all made mistakes on that track today." She glanced at Tyrone in the back of the bus.

"You ran your anchor leg in a new high-school record time of—"

Tyrone could care less. He was looking out the window, searching for Val on every street from Santa Monica all the way back to Watts.

"Stick."

"Take it, Tyrone."

"Don't drop it, anyone."

"Sing to it, brother," Hollywood suggested to Luther. "That's what I do. I sing in my head as I'm carrying the stick."

Hollywood pretended the stick was a microphone. He sang to it in his softest voice.

Luther was too worried to sing.

Ron told Luther to hold the stick like a girl's hand. "You ain't dropping no hand."

When he heard that, Tyrone dropped the stick. The other boys were amazed. But they were too tired to ask Tyrone any questions. Coach Huey had them training harder than ever today.

"Run when you're tired. Pick up and sprint," she called. "When you start to hurt, run faster. Four hundred meters is never pain free. Make it hurt."

"It do!" Ron was gasping.

"Go into the pain. Take command of it," Coach yelled across the track.

Tyrone picked up his pace. The other boys fell off the track and onto the grass. They bent double as far as bodies can bend double. They couldn't believe Tyrone kept sprinting.

"That dude's still a cool breeze," Ron said to his teammates.

Cool? Far from it. Tyrone was hot and tired. But worse than that was the way his hand felt. It felt dead. It felt empty forever. Tyrone ran in order to forget his hand, empty of Val's.

But today he couldn't forget at any speed. He watched his teammates where they lay in the grass. If only he could tell them.

Tyrone ran over there. He couldn't help himself. He stood looking down at them.

"Some girl messed me over," he said in a low voice.

"Who?" Ron asked him right away.

"Hey, what for?" Hollywood asked. He suddenly wanted to hear Tyrone's whole story.

He wouldn't hear it yet because Tyrone bolted for the track again. His teammates lay exhausted.

Then Coach Huey came along and took pity on them. She sent them to the showers.

The three boys quickly changed their clothes and came back to the track, searching for Tyrone. But only the coach was waiting. She had one last lap for them to walk with her.

"In the City Championships, we'll meet Santa Monica again. This time we'll run a record against them," she said.

"Where does Tyrone live?" Luther Junior asked her.

Coach didn't seem surprised by the question. She told Luther that she kept her team records at home. She'd phone him tonight. Then she tried to explain the latest theory about curve running. "Pump your right arm harder than your left. Put more power into your right side on the turn."

For once the boys didn't listen to coaching. They were wondering why some girl—any girl— would mess over the speediest guy in Los Angeles.

8

"Hi. Luther?"

"Yes."

"It's Lynda Huey. I have that address and phone number for you."

"Okay."

"East Watts Street—707 East Watts. Is anything wrong? Is Tyrone injured? A hamstring? Don't tell me he slipped in the shower."

Luther was thinking about injuries. Would you call Tyrone's sad, mean eyes an injury? Or would you say that Tyrone was okay every place *on* his body but that *inside* him Tyrone had this messed-over heart?

Luther decided to find out more before telling coach. "No. Tyrone's fine. What's his phone number?" Luther wrote it down and hung up. He dialed Ron.

"What do you say, man," Ron said. "The lady's name is Valery. Tyrone's lady."

Just like that.

"How'd you find out so soon?" Luther almost dropped the phone in surprise.

"I ask Wanda," said Ron. "She ask around. Some dudes in other schools. She on the phone till she find out Tyrone from L.A. High School. He ran track but he wasn't nothing there. He didn't

have no speed. He left L.A. High when his lady wasted him."

"We got his address now. Maybe we should go over there."

"Yeah," Ron said. "Take him a new lady. If he be strung out behind that Valery, he might flip and disappear on us. Quit the team."

"We can't let him quit before City Championships."

"Deneen say—" Ron began.

"Let's talk to Tyrone." Luther stopped him.

"Take Hollywood over with us. Hollywood sing, dance, make Tyrone laugh." Ron laughed at his own idea.

"Hang up and I'll call Hollywood. Check you later." Luther dialed. He let the phone ring until Hollywood had time to come from any mirror in his house. He didn't answer.

Luther dialed Ron again. And, are you ready for this—? Ron already had a photo of Valery.

"Francie brung it over. It's cut out of the L.A. High yearbook. Valery's a fine, fine lady."

"Tell me about her eyes."

"They brown."

"No, what are they like? Sad? Mean? Nice?"

"Man, you doctors!" Ron fell out laughing. He dropped the spike he'd been holding. "You be looking in folks' eyes for secrets. Next you try to listen to Tyrone's heart!"

That caught Luther by surprise again. But he didn't drop the phone. He held on to it, thinking of how a phone was like a doctor's stethoscope for listening to hearts. He should phone Tyrone and listen to his side of the Valery story. After that, the teammates could figure some way to keep Tyrone's speed on their team.

"Later," Luther said to Ron and hung up.

He dialed Tyrone. "This is Luther. Okay if I come on over to see you?"

No answer from Tyrone.

"Me and Ron and Hollywood, we've been wanting to talk to you about what you said at practice today."

"I was just jiving."

"Could we drive on over anyway?"

"I'm going running." Tyrone's voice sunk lower.

"Could we drive on over early tomorrow morning?"

Tyrone's answer sounded as if it were coming from Kenya, it was so faint. "I run in the mornings. From when I wake up until school."

Luther was stumped. He didn't have another question handy, and anyway Tyrone hung up.

Luther dialed Hollywood. "Meet me and Ron

at 707 East Watts Street tomorrow morning while it's still dark. Maybe five thirty. Wear your sweats and warm-up shoes."

"You for real? I need my beauty sleep. I'm on the couch now, grabbing a few winks while I talk to you."

"Be there." Luther dialed Ron and told him the same thing.

"Five thirty? That's dead."

"We'll run alongside Tyrone for a change. Talk him around—we'll listen him around. We'll listen for how to help him." Luther's ear was already hot from the telephone pressing it.

It would be hotter tomorrow.

At dawn, two sleepy boys waited at Watts Towers, across the street from Tyrone's house. They were dressed for a run.

Little did they know how far.

"We gotta hope he ain't fixing to run as fast as usual," Ron said. He was shot from the night before.

Luther rubbed his eyes. Ron yawned. Finally Hollywood arrived. Then they reviewed their plan to listen to Tyrone. They'd let him blab until he got rid of the hurt that made him into one big fist.

"I hears him coming," Ron whispered.

Tyrone walked out of his house with his shoes in one hand. He sat on the lawn to put them on. Soon, without a stretch, he set off running west.

A block behind him ran three teammates, their feet skimming the quiet streets. They wanted to let Tyrone go a ways before surrounding him.

A mile passed. Two miles. "Let's make our move," said Hollywood.

Luther said, "We'll rap to him first with our feet."

They picked up and came even with Tyrone. He didn't act surprised. He didn't act anything.

"How long you been running like this in the mornings?" Luther asked him.

"Three, going on four months."

Ron said "Since you broke up with your lady. Man, running be more better for you than drownd-ing yourself about Valery."

"I tried that, where I'm running now."

"Where?"

"Pacific."

Hollywood let out his breath in a "Whew." He

said, "Ocean? It's ten miles from here. Slow down so we can hear you."

It was the first time anyone had asked Tyrone to give up speed.

He ran slower. He asked Ron, "How did you find out about Val?"

"It wasn't nothing. Wanda, she say you messed each other over. She ask around."

Tyrone stopped short.

So did the others. They all waited for Tyrone to shoot them down with his eyes.

"We fussed and fought, me and Val. We just didn't say things right, you know?" Tyrone said this in his lowest voice. He started to run again.

"Wait up," called Hollywood when Tyrone got ahead by a block.

Tyrone waited. He moved slowly enough to tell his story. "She used to watch me run at L.A. High. I wasn't so fast. I saw her at the finish line at practice one day. I go up to her and say, 'Hang with me.' I never turned around until we got up top the bleachers."

"Sounds good," Hollywood admitted. He liked this part of L.A. that they were running through now. All these paintings on the walls! Ron and

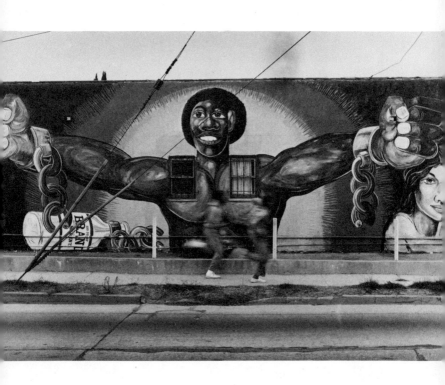

Luther were speeding past huge men with outstretched arms. "Those men are the real Hollywood stars," Hollywood told himself.

Tyrone continued. "I asked what her name
was. She asked, 'Why?' I said, 'Because I don't
kiss girls I don't know the name of.' "

Traffic was picking up. Tyrone waited for a
green light.

"We were tight from then on." Lower, slower,
he said, "We loved each other."

The light changed. Hollywood dropped back. Tyrone ran west toward the Pacific. He passed cars. Behind him a block, Ron called, "I looks at it like this. You be finding a prettier lady soon. We wants to help you find one. Slow up."

"I don't want anyone else," said Tyrone, waiting.

"Even friends?" Luther asked.

"No. Can't care about people. They hurt."

"Why'd you join our team?"

"To learn how to run faster. Speed helps me forget. Coach helps with all her sprints. That race against Coach Huey down Sunset—I never thought of Val."

But now Tyrone was running slowly. And he was thinking of Val. He saw her walking toward him, dancing up next to him, driving past in a car. He remembered out loud how she once borrowed his car and then wrecked it. She said the only reason she'd hit that pole was she couldn't drive straight for thinking of him. Tyrone forgave her. Like she forgave his moods until she couldn't any longer.

Halfway from Watts to the ocean, Hollywood said his legs were gone.

"Heavy as bar-bells." He had to catch a taxi back to where he'd left his car in Watts.

Ron hung on another mile. "This be like running barefooted. These streets is too tough on my dogs." He turned around to hitchhike.

Luther wasn't giving up yet. He'd been listening to Tyrone's secret pain about Valery. Now he hoped to learn another secret: how Tyrone kept from dropping the stick.

"Your hands—your good hands?" Luther asked. "How did you train them?"

The teammates ran many city blocks before Luther got his answer. He'd never been so tired. He was about to give up and ride the bus back to Watts when Tyrone slowed without being asked.

"I feel," he said. "I always feel what I touch. I feel the stick if I take it. I can't drop what I feel."

Luther thought that over for another block. He thought how he'd never really felt the stick. Was it smooth? Was it warm like these streets? Luther told himself to notice at practice later today.

Tyrone was saying, "My hands connect to my brain. My brain remembers feelings." He touched his forehead. "I remember love. I see Val's face at every finish line."

They were walking now, both of them. Luther found a bus stop and sat down on the bench.

Tyrone moved on alone. The ocean wasn't much further. He felt better because he'd told someone—three someones—how he couldn't stop thinking of Val. She walked beside him now in his memory. The street changed to sand under foot. Tyrone picked up speed and entered the waves that came toward him.

"How do you like us so far?" Hollywood asked Tyrone, the final week of track practice.

Tyrone didn't answer.

"I mean, how do you like us running with you mornings? We listen to your stories about Val. About her clothes, how she ties her green sweater around her shoulders. Oh, and me—I sing when I can catch my breath. I did that song you swore was yours with Val." Hollywood sounded as if he wanted Tyrone to like him.

Ron asked Tyrone, "How about me? I be driving every girl I meet over to your house. Goo-gobs. You be acting like they dogs."

Tyrone gave out with a smile. "Turkeys compared to Val."

"Stick," said Luther, in a perfect pass to Ron.

"Stick" was all you heard around the track for an hour—except bragging. Hollywood said, "If a Santa Monica or Fairfax runner cuts in front of me at the Championships, I'm running right up into him and out his eyeballs."

"We blast their doors off."

Luther passed and passed and passed the stick with Coach Huey watching. "Hold on a split second, until you're sure Ron has it tight," she urged Luther.

Tyrone told Luther, "The stick feels alive, like part of your own hand. Pretend you're touching hands, holding hands. Warm up the metal."

Some days Tyrone wasn't around to warm the stick himself. He just didn't show up at the Watts High track. He wouldn't say why.

Coach Huey went easy on him. How could she complain about L.A.'s fastest 400-meter runner? She'd heard of Val by now. She'd overheard the team talking. Also Luther had asked her if she knew a way to cure his teammate's broken heart.

"Tyrone's sad inside," Luther had said. "Tyrone speeds so he can forget this girl he still dreams about when he isn't running with us."

Hollywood chimed in. "But, hey, he's taking the stick with the openest hand on our team now. Notice?"

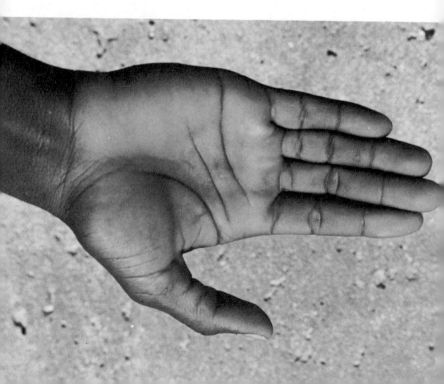

"Even from me," Coach Huey reminded who-
ever wanted to bad-mouth Tyrone.

When Tyrone skipped practice, Coach Huey
hoped he was finding ways to be happy without
running. If he did—and if he quit the team—
they'd lose. Tyrone's speed made her good team
the best in L.A. But she'd rather see smiles from

Tyrone than a trophy or a record. She'd collected enough glory from her own legs when she was a star.

"There's more to life than increasing its speed," Coach Huey said if Luther or Ron or Hollywood grumbled when Tyrone wasn't there to take the stick.

Hollywood wouldn't give up on being a star. "I need that trophy to get my picture taken."

"Speed records are my chance to be a real heart surgeon," Luther confessed to his teammates.

Ron wasn't captain for nothing. He took over their final gripe session with an idea. "I be thinking. One thing our brother need—Val. Check this out. If she at the finish line, Tyrone be there fastest. Ain't that it?"

"Tyrone will fly," said Hollywood.

Luther got suddenly happy. He saw his future self in a doctor's jacket, running down hospital halls. His white coat flew behind him. He saw Tyrone's future self crossing the finish line and jumping into the outstretched arms of a girl waiting there.

Ah, the future.

"What's Valery's last name?" he asked Ron.

"I'll deliver her to the Championships tomorrow."

Hollywood said, "We'll tell her to stay out of sight until the last lap. Then when Tyrone comes around the curve, she'll step out where he can see her—like a movie star."

"Flash on this, brothers. We win with Tyrone. Then every lady in the UCLA stadium get our numbers! Val see how sweet he be." Ron held up a winner's right hand.

Hollywood posed a victory pose. "Let's practice our winning act."

Together, they did.

Here we are at the L.A. City Championships on an early June day. Athletes jog the track, warming up for their races. They wave to friends in the huge crowd. Drake Stadium of UCLA is sold out for this meet.

The Watts High relay team is nowhere to be seen in their blue, gold, and white shirts. Valery is looking for them from her seat near the Watts band. She shades her eyes with a program.

When she finds Ron, she takes three steps down to the track to ask him, "Where shall I wait for Tyrone?"

Ron stays busy tightening his spikes while he
answers. "Near the finish pole. Them judges be
busy studying on their stop watches. They won't
see you slide right on by them."

Hollywood comes jogging along. "Home boy isn't here yet. He didn't ride the team bus."

"You never know about Ty," Valery says to Ron and Hollywood and Luther, who is rubbing the baton. "Ty's moody."

"I feel he'll be here," Luther says. "Also I feel the track. It's a soft rug compared to the others we ran to get this far."

"It's artificial grass made of plastic. Like on professional baseball fields," Coach Huey reminds them all. "Please change over to your short spikes." She turns to Valery. "The team and I are sure glad you've joined us. Tyrone won't let us down. We have another hour yet before our relay."

Valery goes back to her seat. She watches the races when she isn't searching for Ty. She hasn't seen him since February. Will he be taller? Sweeter? Moodier? Will his hair have grown out? He'd cut it when she called it a "nappy mop" as a joke. He'd been so sensitive.

"Final race of this meet, the 1600-meter relay," a voice said on the loudspeaker.

Valery sees Luther already standing by his blocks. He presses the stick against his cheek.

She sees Hollywood take the baton to pat down his hair.

Ron bows to a dozen cheerleaders. He catches Val's eye. He points to the finish pole. Beside it stands the fourth team member, her Tyrone. Tyrone taps each of his brothers on their shoulders. He takes the baton from Luther and gives it a kiss for luck.

"Gun is up!"

Next thing Val knows, Drake Stadium is silent.

Bang.

Luther shoots out of the blocks. He straightens and runs relaxed. He enters the first curve holding the stick like a handful of hand.

Val glances down to where Ty waits for his anchor lap. He's clapping like crazy. When Luther comes into the passing zone and lays the stick in Ron's hand, Ty yells "Beautiful!" above the crowd.

Ron runs his lap in a dream of one girl: Val. She must be one fine lady to come here today to help his team win. Ron wants to get him a lady just like her. "One," he tells himself on the second curve. He's ahead of the other runners: Number One passing the stick to Hollywood.

"Push off each stride," says Hollywood in his head. "Don't try to smile. This is serious. I got to give Tyrone a lead with the stick. His girl's got to see him win. Don't you dare come up on me, Fairfax! Stay back, Santa Monica!"

Only Santa Monica was ahead when Tyrone's hand embraced the stick.

Tyrone ran for his team. They'd listened to his grief. They'd kept him out of the ocean. They'd baked him a custard pie, same as Val used to. They—

Ty couldn't think of all the other help they'd given him lately, because now he was running at top speed. His mind went blank. He blew away Santa Monica and didn't ease up. He wanted to get that record for Coach Huey. She'd taught him speed.

He crosses the finish line without seeing Val at the pole.

But he feels her arms go around him when he bends over to recover his breath.

"I waited for you at the finish line," she whispers.

"What finish line?" Tyrone asks, taking her with the team on their victory lap.

There is no finish line.